❦ BOOK REVIEW

The soft, neatly framed watercolors complement the funny text with the characters' expressive faces and postures, extending the story without overwhelming it. This is a hilarious read-aloud and could prove a turning point in the life of a bossy child—or a mousy one.

from BULLETIN OF THE CENTER FOR
    CHILDREN'S BOOKS

Weekly Reader Children's Book Club presents

A WEEKEND WITH WENDELL

BY KEVIN HENKES

GREENWILLOW BOOKS · NEW YORK

For Nancy and Iggie

This book is a presentation of
Weekly Reader Books.
Weekly Reader Books offers book clubs
for children from preschool through
high school. For further information
write to: **Weekly Reader Books,**
4343 Equity Drive, Columbus, Ohio 43228.

Published by arrangement with
Greenwillow Books.

Library of Congress
Cataloging-in-Publication Data
Henkes, Kevin.
A weekend with Wendell.
Summary:
Sophie does not enjoy energetic,
assertive Wendell's weekend visit
until the very end, when she
learns to assert herself and
finds out Wendell can be
fun to play with after all.
[1. Play—Fiction]   I. Title.
PZ7.H389We 1986 [E] 85-24822
ISBN 0-688-06325-X
ISBN 0-688-06326-8 (lib. bdg.)

The art was prepared as full-color
watercolor paintings combined
with a black pen-and-ink line.
The typeface is Baskerville.

After a snack, Sophie helped Wendell carry his
sleeping bag and suitcase upstairs.

"Well, what are we going to do now?" asked
Wendell. "Do you have any toys?"

Sophie pointed to her toy chest.

"Is that all you've got?" said Wendell. "I've got a
million times more than that. What else is there
to do around here?"

"We could play house?" said Sophie.

"Only if I can make the rules," said Wendell.

On Friday afternoon Wendell's parents dropped him
off at Sophie's house.
"Wendell's going to spend the weekend with us," said
    Sophie's mother, "while his parents visit relatives out of town."
"Oh boy!" said Wendell.
Sophie didn't say anything.

So they played house and Wendell made the rules.
He was the father, the mother, and the five children.
Sophie was the dog.

Then they played hospital.

Wendell was the doctor, the nurse, and the patient.

Sophie was the desk clerk.

When they pretended they worked in a bakery,
Wendell was the baker and Sophie was a sweet roll.
"Isn't this fun?" said Wendell.
Sophie didn't say anything.

At dinner Wendell said that he was allergic to anything
green—so he didn't have to eat his vegetables.
And then, when Sophie wasn't looking, he scooped the
whipped cream off her dessert.

"When is Wendell leaving?" whispered Sophie.

"Soon," said her mother.

"Soon," said her father.

After Sophie's parents tucked Sophie in her bed, zipped
Wendell in his sleeping bag, kissed them both, and
turned off the light, Wendell grabbed his flashlight and
shone it right in Sophie's eyes.
"SEE YOU TOMORROW!" he said smiling.

Sophie shut her eyes. "I can't wait for Wendell to go home," she said to herself.

On Saturday morning, when Sophie woke up, there was a lumpy blue monster jumping up and down on her bed. It was Wendell.

She felt something pinch her leg at breakfast.
It was Wendell.

She heard scary noises coming from the broom closet.
It was Wendell.

Wendell used Sophie's crayons and left them on the
porch so they melted.

At lunch Wendell finger-painted with his
peanut butter and jelly.
"Isn't this fun?" said Wendell.
Sophie didn't say anything.

"When is Wendell leaving?" whispered Sophie.

"Soon," said her mother.

"Soon," said her father.

At bedtime, when Sophie put her head on her pillow, she heard something crunch. It was a note from Wendell. It said, "SEE YOU TOMORROW!" Sophie shut her eyes. "I can't wait for Wendell to go home," she said to herself.

Before Wendell's parents picked him up on Sunday
morning, he tried to make a long-distance call,

and he gave Sophie a new hairdo with shaving cream.

he wrote his name on the bathroom mirror
with toothpaste,

"Want to go outside to help me wash this off?" asked
Sophie. "We could play fire fighter."
"Oh boy!" said Wendell.

So they played fire fighter—and *Sophie* made the rules.
She was the fire chief. Wendell was the burning building.
"Isn't this fun?" said Sophie.
Wendell didn't say anything.

"Do I get to be the fire chief?" asked Wendell.

"Maybe," said Sophie.

Soon Wendell and Sophie didn't care who was
the fire chief or who was the burning building.

"Time to go!" said Sophie's mother.

"Time to go!" said Sophie's father.

"Already?" said Wendell.

"Already?" said Sophie.

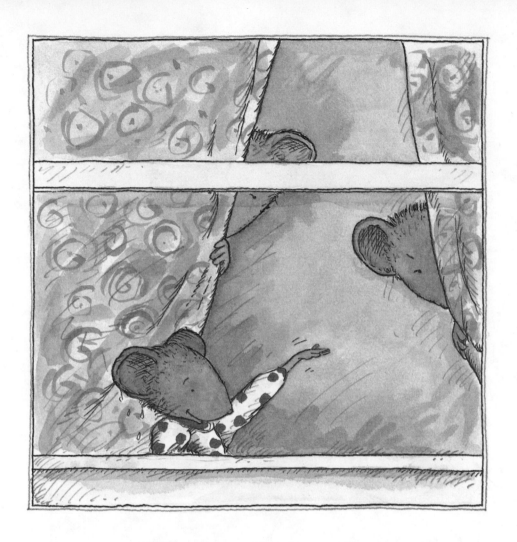

"When is Wendell coming back?" asked Sophie.

"Never!" said her mother.

"Never!" said her father.

That afternoon, when Wendell unpacked his suitcase,
he heard something crunch. It was a note from Sophie.
It said, "I HOPE I SEE YOU SOON!"